Compassion & Consequence

Note: Sale of this book without a cover may be unauthorized. If this book was purchased without a cover, it may have been reported to the publisher as "unsold or destroyed." Neither the author nor the publisher may have received payment for the sale of this book.

This novel is a work of fiction. Any resemblance to real people either living or dead, actual events, establishments, organizations or locale are intended to give the fiction a sense of reality and authenticity and is entirely coincidental. Other names, characters, places or incidents are either products of the author's imagination or are used fictitiously as are those fictitious events & incidents that involve real persons and did not occur or are set in the future.

Published by: Kweli Legacy, LLC
ISBN: 9798681927389
Copyright © 2019
Printed in the USA

Compassion for Christmas

by Nikkea Sharee

1

The winter chill pierced through the clothing that attempted to cover the elderly man's flesh. He could see his breath start to freeze and turn into a smoke before his very eyes. Still, it was not as cold as his heart.

Winter was Caleb's least favorite season. It was a constant reminder that he was alone and would probably be alone for the rest of his life. Years earlier the only love that he had ever known had passed away on Christmas day. He remembered vividly holding his wife's cold hand as he sat next to her bedside praying for her to get well. There was a very specific moment when he felt the energy in the room shift.

Down the hall he could hear people attempting to spread good cheer through holiday songs. His wife loved the holidays; he had never imagined she would have her last breath on Christmas day. He felt her hand go numb, heard her last breath leave her body. It was at that moment that his spirit was forever broken.

Years had passed and Caleb remained in a bahumbug mood every time the season came about. Christmas. The same holiday that seemed to bring so many so much joy brought him nothing but disdain. And for that very reason, he decided that he would do something totally out of character. Something so stupid that he would have never done anything like this had his wife been alive. But she wasn't, and there was no one to talk him off of the ledge. He was alone in a world full of Christmas cheer, but a grinch nonetheless.

Christmas, in his opinion, was all about the commercialism. As soon as Halloween was over, in came commercials promoting propaganda to get people to buy things to make their loved ones happy. Caleb however knew the truth. No matter how much one bought for their loved ones during the holiday season, they couldn't take it with them when they died.

Snow began to fall around him as he stood in front of the grocery store. They had closed hours ago but what he had come for was staring in his face. He had come up with the idea earlier in the day when he had gone to the same grocery story to stock up on food. Walking out he noticed the display just outside the doors.

Christmas trees.

They were leaning on top of each other haphazardly. The scraggily looking things had needles that were browning, in desperate need of water. He felt bad for them. The way that the trees were discarded in front of the building reminded him of how he felt on the inside. Slowly decaying. It was in that moment that he decided that he was going to bring one of them home.

Only he had no intention of purchasing a tree. That would only feed into the commercialism that this holiday was all about. No, that wouldn't work at all. He was going to steal a tree.

The thought of doing something so foolish actually made him giddy. It had been years since the man had done anything even remotely on the edge. For the most part, Caleb lived an honest life, but there was a stint in his youth when he had done some things that he never imagined he would do again. But there he was in the middle of the night standing in front of a heap of Christmas trees, ready to steal one.

The tree didn't need to be big. In his mind he thought about the Charlie Brown Christmas movie and how much his late wife loved it. As he stood in the arctic cold weather, his mind took a small trip to the last time they watched the movie together. It was in the hospital. She was weak but alert. A smile would spread across her face in a way that he wanted to hold on to it forever.

It was in that spirit that Caleb wanted to bring a tree home, albeit a small one and hoist it up in her memory. Carolyn never would have permitted him to steal anything for her. And there was no doubt that he could afford to pay for it. He just didn't want to. Didn't feel as though he needed to. There was no way that he would feed into the commercialism of the holiday. He just wanted to take a tree, go home and pour some liquor to sip on as he played her favorite music until he passed out.

In the morning he would laugh at how silly this entire caper had been and eventually throw the tree away. But first, he needed to commit the heist.

His adult mind was starting to kick in. This was stupid. Dumb. He didn't need a tree. Why steal one? Second guessing everything about what he was doing started to curve his mind. It wasn't too late. He could just go home. Leave this foolish decision in the spot where he stood and go home to be alone.

There was no real reason that he had to do this. What if he got caught? This was a Christmas tree, not a piece of candy that he was planning to steal. The grocery store had to have some type of security to leave the trees out at night with no supervision. This was ridiculous, his mind settled on. It was time for him to go surely. Enough was enough. He had lived out his silly childhood ways long enough and this was no way to honor Carolyn.

Turning on his heels to leave Caleb was startled by the presence of someone else. He was not alone.

2

"What are you doing?"

Caleb looked down at the figure before him. What the hell was going on? It was the dead of the night and here was a child standing in front of him that couldn't be older than seven.

"Where did you come from? Do you know what time it is? You shouldn't be out here by yourself. Have you run away from home?"

Confusion flooded Caleb's mind as he looked at the child. He then searched the parking lot for somewhere the child could have come from. It was cold, too cold for him let alone a child.

"I don't have to answer you. You need to answer me. What are you doing? Are you going to steal a Christmas tree? Are you a grinch or something?"

Caleb couldn't help but laugh at the innocence of the child and the line of questions that were being thrown at him like daggers. The child reminded him of himself when he was younger, all spunk and crass. He still didn't understand why the child was alone in the middle of the night.

"No, I'm not going to steal a tree. I was just looking at them. But where are your parents? Are you out here alone?"

The child stared at him with a very blank expression on his face. His mother had told the child not to talk to strangers. But this wasn't a stranger right. This was a burglar. And burglars were bad guys. Only there was no one around to protect the trees but the child, so he had to intervene.

"You are under citizens arrest! Put your hands up!" The child looked up with a very serious gaze. One hand resting on his hip, the other held up like a stop sign. He would have pointed at the man like a gun, but he also had been told that he was too young for a gun, so despite his dream of growing up to become a police officer, the child had to settle for being a security guard in his mind. Either way, he was very serious about not allowing any miscarriage of justice to happen on his watch.

"Kid, come on. I told you I was not going to steal a tree." This of course was only a half truth. He had only changed his mind about the caper moments before being discovered by the child. Neither one of them were giving up their position.

"I said freeze, mister!"

"Jonathan! What are you doing out here!" Out of seemingly nowhere a woman appeared. "Oh my gosh, I'm so sorry. I hope he isn't bothering you."

Caleb didn't know what to say, from the child who had interrupted his midnight heist to the woman who had come to his rescue, things were happening quicker than he could comprehend.

"Mom, no you don't understand. This man was going to steal a tree. I had to save them! I had to save the trees."

Embarrassed, Caleb attempted to save himself, "I wasn't going to steal a tree."

"Yes, you were. I watched you! The store is closed and you've been standing in front of the trees for an hour."

"Jonathan, I told you to stay in the car. You don't come out ever without me. And you certainly don't go roaming around at midnight. Anything could have happened to you. It's a miracle I woke up, but you scared me half to death."

It was at that moment that Caleb noticed a car parked in the far side of the parking lot. He didn't know why he hadn't noticed it before. But there it was, parked, partially covered with snow. From the snow on the ground in front of it, he could tell that the car had not been moved in sometime. They couldn't have been living in that car. It had to be every bit of thirty degrees outside and while the child appeared to have been well bundled, there was no way that he could fathom the mother and child were actually living in the vehicle.

"Uh mom! How am I ever going to learn how to be an awwwwficer if I don't practice." The child looked very upset that his mother had hindered his plans to complete his first citizens arrest. He didn't comprehend the danger that he could have been in if Caleb was someone else.

The world was much more dangerous than it had been when Caleb was growing up. Even with that, as a child he knew better than to approach a stranger let alone in the dead of night. He watched as the woman collected her child as she chastised him.

His mind was a blur, looking from the car to the pair and back all while snow fell around them. Finally, he felt how truly cold it was outside. This was no condition for anyone let alone a woman and a child. He couldn't wrap his mind around what may have led them to these living conditions, but he knew he had to do something.

"Ma'am, its really ok. My name is Caleb by the way," He extended his hands in the direction of the woman in an attempt to greet her politely.

The flush look on her face told him everything that he needed to know. She was in mom defense mode. Her only goal was to protect her child. "Hi, umm Rebecca. And this is Jonathan. Again, I hope we didn't interrupt too much of your night. My son has a huge imagination."

Jonathan dropped his eyes to the ground no longer wanting to look up and make eye contact. Caleb knew this look; it was the look of a spirit broken. This was not anything he wanted to be a part of and needed to find a way to make it right.

In that moment he realized that no matter how bad he thought that he had it in life, this family had by far trumped him. Even the pain of losing his wife seemed to take a literal back seat to him seeing this woman walk her son back to a chilly car during the worst weather condition seasons. He couldn't just stand there and do nothing.

"Rebecca," running up behind them Caleb didn't really know what he was going to say that would possibly make a difference in their situation.

The woman turned around slowly while clutching her son's hand tightly. She was visibly scared. She didn't know what this man's motives would be and desperately needed to protect her son, which she would do even if it took her last breath.

"Yes?" Slightly she tucked her son behind her. The truth was, it was after midnight. This was a stranger. She and her son were alone. She didn't know what this man's motives were.

"Uhhh, I heard you say something about your car. I don't know how to say this any other way so I apologize if I'm being intrusive, but you all aren't living in your car are you?"

Hearing the man state the obvious aloud made her cringe. She had been very careful on how she explained what was happening to her son. Yes, they had fallen on hard times. Technically they were homeless, but her son did not know what that mean. He didn't know how far into rock bottom they had hit. Her son had a grand imagination and she had been very careful to take care of him in a way that he didn't know what was really happening to them, how destitute they really were.

However, hearing the man say it aloud caused a punch to her gut. She hadn't felt defeated before that moment. She had felt as though she had done the best she could for her child without having to give him up to child protective services. No, she would protect her child the best she could. Sensing danger, she started to move her and her child quicker to their car. Once there she would drive away from this man, hopefully never to see him again.

"I'm sorry, we've got to go!" She said before taking Jonathan's hand to run faster to the car. She could not risk this man calling the authorities on her that night. Her son didn't understand what his actions could have triggered, but she did. And she was trying all she could to keep them afloat.

"Wait, I don't want to hurt you. I just..." Caleb's voice trailed off as he attempted to run behind them. He wasn't the man he used to be, and catching the pair was not likely going to happen as he tripped over something in the snow and fell headfirst onto the pavement. He felt the cold of the ground before blacking out, something he hadn't done in a long time.

3

Hearing a thud behind them, Jonathan turned to look back at the man. "Mom, momma, moooooommmm!" He cried out as his mother nearly dragged him back to the car.

She didn't listen as she threw him into the passenger side of the vehicle. Rushing to the other side, she fumbled with her keys in a haste to start the car.

"You're not listening. We've got to help him!" Jonathan was persistent and in tears as he begged for his mother to pay attention to him.

"What baby? We have to go. Don't' you understand?"

"No mom, the man! He fell in the snow. We have to help him."

Looking over in the direction of where she had fled from the man, she noticed a figure in the snow. Cursing in her head loudly, she hit the steering wheel in frustration. Why hadn't her son stayed in the car? He was asleep before she fell asleep. Why had he woken up and found this man in the middle of the night? She didn't want to think about what he was doing there. She just wanted to get her son far away from anything that may put them in harms way.

However, now seeing the lump face down in the cold snow she felt as though she needed to do something. Surely she could not leave the man there by himself. He could freeze to death.

"Lord, I don't know what to do," she spoke aloud to no one in particular. These days she had been doing that more frequently than less when she felt out of her control. For the most part she was able to keep things together. At the moment she was falling apart.

Jonathan was looking as though he was scared out of his mind for this man, "I hope he's not dead."

"No baby, he's not dead." She hoped her words were true as she got out of the car to inspect things closer. "Stay put."

Walking back over to the man, Rebecca wished that she had a cell phone where she could call for help. The only problem with that was she had to make a decision to get gas and food for them and could not afford to pay the bill. There were no payphones even existent like there had been years ago when she was growing up. The world revolved around cellular phones and there she was without one in an emergency situation.

Leaning down to check the man's pulse, she could see that he was still alive and let out a sigh of relief. He must have just passed out when he hit the concrete.

"Is he dead?"

"Jonathan! Oh my gosh, you scared me. I thought I told you to stay in the car."

"I wanted to help. It's my civic duty."

Rebecca prayed her son would not turn out to be the end of her as she struggled to understand his inquisitive nature. As innocent as her son was, without his mischievousness that evening, none of this would have happened.

"Ok baby, I know, and you will be a great civic leader one day, but right now we need to make sure this man is ok."

"We can't call the ambulance for him, can we?" Jonathan was thinking hard on what they may be able to do.

"No baby, mommy's phone isn't working."

"I know. We can take him home."

"Baby, I don't think we need to move him if he is out of it. I'm not a medical professional."

"We can't leave him here."

"I know baby, I know. Just give momma a minute to think please." Her patience was wearing thin. More than anything she wanted to get her son far away. But she couldn't help but think of how bad she would disappoint him if she were to leave the man lying there in the cold. It was simply too cold outside. She couldn't live with herself if the man froze to death because she didn't try to help.

"Where is your car, Mr. Caleb? Maybe if I could get you to your car…"

"He walked."

"What?"

"The man. He walked from that way," her son pointed at nothing in particular, just the edge of the shopping complex which led to a street heading in the direction of a residential neighborhood. "I saw him when he walked up. That's what made me watch him to make sure he didn't steal the trees."

Now she knew her son's mind was wandering. If the man had walked up, how could he possibly think he could leave with a tree. Now wasn't the time to explain that logic to her child. She just needed to figure out her next steps. "Ok, ok, ok.... Think Rebecca."

"We should drive him home mom. If he is not dead like you said, we should drive him home."

"He's not dead but I don't know if he needs some other type of medical help."

"Moooom check his pockets. Maybe he has a wallet or something."

Digging in the man's pockets, she realized that her son may have been on to something. Not only did she find a wallet, but she also found keys to what she hoped was his home.

"See, now once we get home, we can call the ambulance and make sure he is ok." Her son was a genius. She smiled at the young boy and touched the top of his head, brushing his hair lightly.

"Can you stay here with the man while I get the car and bring it over?"

Jonathan shook his head up and down. This was like an adventure to him. First, he had saved the trees. Now he was saving a life. On most nights when he woke up in the middle of the night when his mom was asleep, he only acted like he was a superhero. Tonight, he was getting a chance to be one.

Rushing back to the car, Rebecca swiftly turned it on and put it in gear. She pulled up as closely as she could to the man and her son. Jumping out of the car with it still running, she opened the door to the back and with Jonathan's help, put the man in the back of her car. Praying that she was doing the right thing, she looked at the address on the license and drove in that direction.

One good thing about her situation was that she was like a human gps as she drove around many days and therefore didn't need the help of a device to figure out how to get to the man's home. She had been employing survival techniques ever since she and her son had become homeless. If there was one thing she knew, it was how to get around and how to survive.

Thankfully the man's home was in walking distance to the grocery store and she could understand why he may have walked. She parked directly in front of the small colonial and looked around. It was such a nice neighborhood. She silently prayed that one day she and her son could live in such a home as this.

But there was no time to daydream. She had an unconscious man in her backseat. Her heart was beating a million miles a minute. What if he didn't live alone and someone thought she was breaking into the house? What if he had a massive pit bull or rottweiler that would attack them. So many thoughts raced through her mind as she debated her next steps. She wished that she could be anywhere but here. Why her? All she wanted was to make it through the night safely with her son. It was a simple prayer she had prayed every night. And every night with a boisterous young boy it seemed harder and harder to achieve.

"Mom, he's moving." Jonathan had kept a close eye on the man once he had been placed in the back seat so that his mother could drive in peace. That was short lived. The man was starting to come to.

"Oh thank God, sir! Sir! Mr. Caleb, are you alright?"

Caleb's head felt like he was hit by a sledgehammer. This wasn't a scenario he was new to. "I think so, just a little weak. Where am I?"

"We brought you home!" Jonathan shouted with glee.

Rebecca remembered that she had taken the man's wallet and keys out. "I'm sorry, I don't have a phone and didn't know what else to do. We were going to take you home and try to call you an ambulance. Here is your wallet and keys. We didn't take anything out. We just wanted to get you home safely."

Sitting up in the backseat of the car, Caleb rubbed his head. "Thank you. I think I've got it from here. No need to call emergency."

Attempting to step out of the car by himself, the man stumbled a bit on the ground. Rebecca rushed out of the car to help the man. "If you don't mind, let us help you in. It's the least we can do for my son bothering you."

"I wasn't bothering him and you are still under citizens arrest, mister."

"Jonathan, stop it. How was he going to get a Christmas tree home and he didn't even drive there?"

"He was going to take the little one, like in Charlie Brown Christmas. I saw him staring at it."

"I'm sorry sir. Let's get you in the house."

"You are going to be a very good police officer one day young man," Caleb announced not quite confirming that he was in fact there to steal a tree.

"I know!" Jonathan said as he helped the man walk up to his front door.

Caleb fumbled with his keys before passing them to Rebecca. "The one with the orange top please."

She did as suggested and helped the man with opening the door. Inside there was no big barking dog. No family members to greet them. Just a television flickering in the distance which had been muted. The man's home was very clean, almost too clean. It was as though no one lived there at all. Everything was put into its perfect place. Something she couldn't do if she tried with a child like Jonathan. He was always getting into something, even in the small quarters of a car.

"Well glad you are feeling better. I think it's best we leave now."

"Ma'am, it's the middle of the night. Why don't you and your son come in and get warmed up. I think I have some hot chocolate in the kitchen. I promise I'm not an axe murderer and if I can recall I'm under citizens arrest. I can't get into any more shenanigans tonight."

"Can we please mom?" Jonathan seemed to jump up and down with excitement.

Rebecca was walking a thin line. How could she not disappoint her son while protecting him at the same time. She turned behind her to look at the snow that seemed to have picked up speed. It was a cold night. They had been sleeping in the car for weeks and she could no longer afford to rent a hotel for them. She stayed away from shelters out of fear that they would see her as an unfit mother and take her son away from her. Jonathan had no idea the things she did to sacrifice for them. He was a child. He couldn't understand.

Yet here they were, in the middle of a snowy night, inside of a stranger's house. But at this point were they really strangers? Her son had arrested the man. They then saved him from potential hypothermia. That had to count for something didn't it?

"Ok, but we won't be staying long. So you just get that in your head young man, you hear me?"

Jonathan disregarded her and followed the older man into his kitchen as if he owned the place or at least had been there before. Rebecca looked back at her car and made sure it was locked before closing the front door to the home. What a night and it was just getting started.

4

"Your home is beautiful." Rebecca admired the quaint home as she walked throughout on her way to kitchen. She was still very tired. However, the events of the night had definitely woken her up. Her body wanted nothing more than to rest, but alas, the energy that her son had would not make that possible. She knew that as long as he was up, she would need to be up if for nothing more than to watch over him.

"Thank you. This is more company than I've had in a long time so please excuse the mess." Caleb was a very particular man. Everything had a place and he always kept things in their place. His wife had been the one that started the couple on a lifestyle of absolute cleanliness. It made his heart feel more connected to her by keeping things neat and in their place.

"You have to be kidding right? I never have been in a home so neat and tidy." Rebecca looked around taking it all in. She missed having a home, somewhere that she could go to every night. She enjoyed taking a moment for her and her son to be in from the cold, even if it was just a moment.

"I normally don't like to sleep without doing the dishes. I'm a bit embarrassed about it. Imagine the one time I don't clean the kitchen all the way. I guess tonight I wasn't in the right mental space."

"Is that why you were going to steal the Christmas tree mister?" Jonathan sat on a high stool at the kitchen island which allowed his feet to swing freely.

Rebecca's face started to get flush. As much as she loved her son, sometimes she wished that he didn't say the very first thing on his mind. It was times like these that she wanted to crawl into a cave. "I'm so sorry Caleb. My son has a huge imagination. I'm sure you weren't out there to steal a Christmas tree."

Caleb walked over to the stove just as the teapot signaled that the water was just hot enough. Taking the pot off of the hot stove he then walked over to the cupboard and retrieved a few cups, saucers and spoons. Preparing the hot chocolate and topping it off with marshmallows, he served his guests.

"In this instance, I'm afraid your inquisitive son is correct. I was there to steal a Christmas tree. Well I was going to at first but changed my mind. I had no idea that my plans would be discovered by a child in the middle of the night. You are going to be very good young man."

"But why mister? Why were you going to steal the Christmas tree?"

Caleb never knew a question so simple could be so triggering and that from a child. He felt ashamed of his initial motives that night; however, somehow he felt as though it was serendipitous. For if he had not gone out that night determined to steal a tree, he never would have had the opportunity to get this family out of the frigid cold.

"My late wife, her name was Carolyn, she used to love watching A Charlie Brown Christmas. She passed away a few years ago, on Christmas day. Ever since then I haven't been in the spirit much. Heck, I think this holiday has become all about who can spend the most money on each other. It's not about the spirit of giving or spending time with family. When my wife died I realized just how much the little things matter. That little tree simply reminded me of her. But then I realized she never would have wanted me to do something so foolish. And I was just about to leave when little Jonathan here arrested me."

Rebecca had never heard of anything so sad. Losing a loved one on Christmas day. From what she could see, he had lived alone since Carolyn's passing. She regretted her son intervening on the man's small and simple caper. He just wanted to be connected to his wife again. She could certainly understand that. In fact, if there was anyone in the world who could understand missing a loved one around the holidays it was her.

Dropping her head for a moment she was at a loss for words. For weeks she had focused on her dire situation that she hadn't thought about the millions of other people in the world who were also going through hard times.

"I'm sorry I arrested you mister. I was just trying to save the trees." Jonathan's sweet face looked up at the man with huge puppy dog eyes. Finishing up his hot chocolate the young boy opened his mouth for a deep yawn.

Seeing how tired her son was, Rebecca decided that it was time to leave the man to his space. "Caleb, thank you for your kindness. We should be leaving now."

"Nonsense. There is still snow coming down pretty hard and the temperatures are not coming up any higher before the morning. You and Jonathan are more than welcome to stay for the night. I have three bedrooms in this house and use for only one. It's the least I can do for you saving my life."

"I didn't save your life."

"Rebecca, you are being modest. If you hadn't brought me home, I may have still been laying in the freezing snow for who knows how long. I promise you I'm not an ax murderer, plus if I am, I'm certain Jonathan will arrest me again," Caleb chuckled.

For the first time that night they all joined in a hearty laugh. "I guess, since you put it that way, and this boy obviously is determined to fall asleep right here. I'll tell you one thing, his weight when sleeping is like a grown man."

"Let me carry him for you. I think you've carried enough grown men for the night."

5

The sun flooded the room causing Rebecca to wake abruptly from her sleep. She lay on top of the sheets while her son was nestled closely to her still fast asleep. The events from the prior night started to enter her memory bank.

Her eyes started to flood as she thought about the kindness of the stranger they met by pure coincidence. She felt bad that she had nothing to offer the man in return but grateful that she and her son had shelter from the cold.

There were so many times where she felt as though life simply was not fair to her. Her upbringing was one that she didn't share with anyone. The truth was there wasn't anything to share. She had been raised by an older aunt who never spoke of her birth parents. It was like she was some sort of bad family secret that no one wanted to discuss. In fact, most of her family acted as though she didn't exist at all. So when she turned eighteen, she sought out independence in hopes of finding something, anything that was better than the way she grew up.

What Rebecca had come to find out was that adulthood was just as bad as a neglected childhood. She struggled to keep steady work, building credit proved to be difficult and the only thing she truly owned was the car that she and her son now lived in.

Jonathan. He was the only light to her dim world. The product of a one-night affair with a man she had met who had come home on a military leave. She just knew that when she met Jonathan's father her life would change for the better. Not that she was looking for someone to save her, but he was absolutely a silver lining of hope. A moment of happiness in a life riddled with unfortunate events.

Alas, the man she had met and spent one magical night with promised her that he was being called out to service. He wished that he would be able to stay with her, but told her that when his tour of duty was over, he would find her. Only, he never did. Instead she received a letter from a friend of his saying that her beau had died in combat. In the letter the man did say how highly he had spoken of her and how much he wanted to be with her. The letter was bittersweet. On one hand she knew that there would have been a future, if only he lived to make it back to the states. On the other hand, he would never know that he fathered a child with her that they conceived on the night they spent together.

Still, Rebecca allowed zero time for her emotions to get the best of her. She raised her son as though his father was right there with her and told him stories of the hero that his father was. Jonathan had something to be proud of, a father that had character and was strong and...

...was sitting in a picture frame on the dresser of the room she was now resting in. Rebecca jumped up as softly as she could without alarming her son of her movement. This couldn't be right? Even though she had only seen her child's father the day they first met, she always remembered every inch of him. In fact, they had taken a picture at a photo booth together that she had held onto all of those years.

Retrieving the photo from a pocket inside of her wallet, she walked over to the picture that was on the dresser to compare the two. It was definitely him. Suddenly she felt a sense of eeriness. How could she explain this? How could anyone explain this? Was the man who had welcomed her and her son into his home the night before somehow related to the father of her child? This was starting to become too much for her, but her mind simply would not wrap around what was staring her right in front of her face.

Rebecca knew that she could not leave that house until she got the answers that she needed. This would be an uncomfortable but necessary moment for both her and the older gentleman. She absolutely had to confirm if her suspicions were true.

Walking out of the bedroom softly as not to wake her son, Rebecca made her way down the hallway. She could already smell breakfast cooking in the kitchen which meant that Caleb was awake. This would be a good time to ask the questions that where swarming her mind without interruption from her sweet yet inquisitive son.

"Good morning, I hope my tinkering in the kitchen didn't wake you. I don't know if you are hungry, but I figured before you got on your way, you and your son could join me for a meal." The man had been busy all morning working on a spread that could rival that of a five-star hotel. She was impressed by his level of hospitality.

"Thank you so much, but you didn't have to go through all this trouble." She was overwhelmed with emotion from both the questions that she needed to ask the man as well as his kind gesture. Breakfast for her and her son lately had been down to the bare essentials. She kept cereal in the car and would get single servings of milk from the grocery store each morning for them to eat. Caleb had prepared more food than she had seen in what seemed like ages.

"Yes, I did. And I hope that you don't decline my offer. Did you sleep well?" Caleb switched the topic of conversation.

"It was fine, Jonathan may have enjoyed it more than me. He's still asleep. You have to forgive us in advance if we overstay our welcome. We will be out of your hair as soon as we wake up fully and get going."

"Listen, I know I'm still very much a stranger to you and your son, but I'm not rushing you. I hate to ask this but, do you and your son really live in your car?"

She knew that the question about her living situation would eventually come up. Had attempted to prepare her mind for the inevitable. But there simply was no way around it. "Yes, just until I get on my feet." At least that's what she had told herself time and time again. Only it was hard to do so with no home address, no working phone, no childcare. Her options had long ago run thin. Only defeat was not an option she was wiling to accept.

Caleb stopped what he was doing for a moment to take the young woman in. This was his first time actually looking at the younger woman. He immediately felt empathy for her. There were so many questions he had about her situation, but he didn't want to scare her off.

"I wont ask you more than you may be comfortable divulging, but I am curious where is your family. Is there no one who could take you in?"

There was so much she could have said and so little that she wanted to say at the same time. Her life, her history, it was no walk in the park. "For lack of better words, I don't have a family. I only have Jonathan. It's been he and I since he was born." For reasons she could not understand, it was easier talking to this man about her past than she thought.

"I understand." Caleb thought about his own extended family. After his wife's funeral, all of the people that claimed he could call on them if ever he needed anything seemed to disappear. Kind words were all that was left. Phone calls had long stopped. Visits were nonexistent. He was used to solitude; it was the time that he needed to heal his wounds. The years that he spent alone only seemed to make him more indifferent toward them.

"Caleb, can I ask you a question?" She watched as he flipped pancakes on a griddle. If nothing else Jonathan would be excited when he woke up for the pancakes alone.

"Sure, shoot." Caleb wanted to know more about his house guest, but didn't want to push. Keeping her talking would be a good way for him to learn more, so he could see how he could be of assistance. He had made up in his mind that he would help the small family and was about to announce so right before he had fallen in the snow. As fate would have it, he would have a chance to get to know them after all.

"Who's room was it that we slept in last night?" That question, while innocent caused him to pause for just a moment. The only subject that was more sensitive for him to discuss than his wife was his late son, Patrick.

"It was my son's room." The word 'was' hung in the air like clothes that needed to be air dried after washing.

Immediately Rebecca felt bad for asking, but she also knew she needed to get down to the bottom of her mystery. When Caleb said his son's name, she knew that there were only so many things that were coincidence. Patrick was the name of the man she had fallen in love with at first sight years before.

"Is this your son?" Rebecca slid the photo strip taken at a booth the night she and Patrick united over to Caleb. She had just about all the confirmation she needed, but this would be the tell-tale sign.

Caleb stopped what he was doing to look at what Rebecca was handing him. The photo strip was old, worn and small in scale. However, there was no denying it was his son. He could point out his son in a sea of people. What he couldn't make sense of was how this woman he just met had a picture of his son.

"Yes, this is Patrick. How did you know him? He died before my wife. Had to be at least seven years ago."

Rebecca sat down in the closest chair. She needed to balance herself. This was all happening way too fast. The room was starting to spin.

Caleb rushed around the island to help Rebecca as she stumbled into the seat. "I'm sorry. I hope I didn't upset you. Are you ok?"

"It's not that." Rebecca steadied herself with Caleb's help. Tears started to rush her face. The emotion was coming at her way too fast. "Patrick, was he in the military? Did he die in combat?"

The questions that she asked made him wonder who she really was. Only someone that knew his son could have known that. "Yes, he was and yes that was how he died. But how do you know all of this?"

Rebecca took her time answering him this time. The silence seemed to be fitting for the moment though she knew he was anxious to understand where all of this was coming from and where it was going to. "Patrick, your son. He is Jonathan's father."

One could have bought Caleb for a dollar. Making breakfast was no longer a concern of his. Looking at this woman closer he wondered was this some type of sick joke. "My son didn't have any children. What are you talking about?" His tone rose an octave as he digested what she said.

His son had a son. How could this be?

"I think you may want to turn the stove off. It looks like we have a lot to talk about."

6

Caleb sat at the table nearly dumbfounded after hearing Rebecca recount meeting his son and their love story, no matter how brief. He wondered why he had never heard of her from him and now it was apparent. She hadn't had the opportunity to truly allow their love to blossom. If he didn't believe in love at first sight, he did after she finished.

Tears were hanging on for dear life in the corners of her eyes. This moment was absolutely serendipitous. What were the chances that a fluke encounter would cause her to meet her son's grandfather? Then there was the fact that he had been so kind to them without obligation. In one night, she had been treated better by a stranger than she had been treated by her entire family. She only hoped that what she told him didn't scare him off.

Sitting at the table next to the man who could have very well been her father in law if his son had lived seemed surreal. She felt connected to Patrick more than she ever had since the last time she had seen him. That night was one that she would never forget. This moment was second.

Silently, Rebecca wondered what Caleb was thinking. Would he think that she was crazy and throw her and her son out of his home? Would he want to hear more? Did she have more to tell him? Aside from the night that she had given Patrick all of her contact information down to her home address at the time, she didn't have anything to tell the man.

"Who would have thought that me going out last night to steal a Christmas tree would allow me to meet my... my... grandson!" It was at that moment that she realized that he had tears in his eyes as well. She felt a load lift off of her as she realized that he wasn't upset about the revelation that she told him.

"I'm sorry if I burdened you at all. It's just that when I saw Patrick's picture on the dresser in his room, I just couldn't hold back. I needed to know if what I was seeing was true."

"You are no burden at all. You had no idea who I was and vice versa. I guess this is what one would call destiny. The real question is where do we go from here?"

The question was a loaded one. The last thing that Rebecca wanted to do was intrude on the man's life any more than she already had. "If it's ok with you, Caleb, I think I need to figure out how to explain all of this to my son when he wakes up first."

"Explain what to me?" Jonathan walked into the kitchen still wiping the cold out of the corner of his eyes. He had no idea what it was that he just walked in on.

"Hey baby. Um, Caleb is it ok if we get washed up here before we eat the breakfast you prepared?" Rebecca was so consumed with the revelation that had just taken place that she hadn't heard her son approach them.

"Yes, absolutely. Take all the time that you need."

7

Caleb sat at the kitchen island dumbfounded. There were so many things that were running through his mind. He immediately felt guilty that he had spent so much of his life being bitter by the fact that he was alone in the world only to discover that he had an extended family that were living in impoverished conditions not far away.

As though someone had turned on the fire in his heart the ice that had been taking residence there started to melt. Jonathan had the same spirit that Patrick held when he was younger. The more that the thought about it the more he realized that there was no DNA test that would be needed to prove that they were blood. Walking to a trunk in his bedroom, he retrieved an old photo album. As though he had stepped into a time machine, there he was. Almost a mirror image of the young boy he had met just the night before. This was all the proof he needed. Jonathan was a spitting image of his son at that age.

He was flourished with emotion. This had to be a miracle. If Caleb could have one wish for Christmas, it would be that his newfound family stay with him until they were able to get back on their feet. There was no way that he would allow either one of them to spend one more minute in the streets. They were his responsibility now. And no matter what caused Rebecca to land on the streets, he could see that she was a good person doing the best she could and he would help her any way he could.

"Mr. Caleb, where are you?" Jonathan called from the kitchen. Wiping the tears from his eyes, he could only hope that these pictures would make what they needed to explain to Jonathan a little bit easier to understand. It was hard enough for an adult, but for a child it could be too much to comprehend.

"I'm right here, I just wanted to bring a few things to show you." Caleb walked from his bedroom to the kitchen holding a few items that he hoped would make the young man's day.

"Caleb, we won't be in your hair too much longer. We really thank you for all the hospitality you have shown us this far. Honestly we just wanted to make sure you were ok from last night." Rebecca was still trying to figure things out in her mind let alone how she would break the news to her son.

"Ok you two, have a seat. Let's eat breakfast and chat for a few. You are welcome and now it's my time to tell a story."

Rebecca looked at the man a bit confused by his declaration but followed instructions nonetheless. "Jonathan, can you say grace so we can eat?"

Caleb watched as the young man did his best to sit up at the table with his fingers clasped together. His eyes were slightly cracked so he could marvel at all of the food that sat before him. It was as if her were about to have a long-awaited feast. The young boy could not recall the last time he saw a feast such as this before him. He was excited.

"Dear God, thank you for all this food. Thank you for the warm bed last night. Thank you for saving Mr. Caleb. I'm sorry I arrested him. I was just trying to save the trees. But I hope he gets his tree, he's nice. Thank you for my mom and tell my dad I said hello in heaven. Amen."

Jonathan started to pile his plate up with all the food that he could. In his mind he didn't know the next time that he would eat like this. He loved his mom, but he knew she couldn't afford to feed him like this every day. He saw it as a treat and wanted to enjoy every morsel.

"Slow down baby. The food isn't going anywhere."

"Yes ma'am. So what was it you guys wanted to talk to me about? What is that you brought in here, Mr. Caleb? That book looks really old."

Caleb looked at Rebecca to see if he had permission to proceed with the difficult story they had at hand. "It's a family photo album." Opening to the page that held a picture of Patrick at Jonathan's age, the man sat the book in front of his grandson.

"Wow, he looks just like me!" Jonathan marveled as he looked at the image while shoving a slice of bacon in his mouth. The table exploded with laughter at how candid he was.

"That is my son. His name is Patrick. He is... in heaven."

"Like my daddy?"

"Yes, you see son, your mother and I discovered this morning that my son was your father. And that's what you walked in on us talking about a bit ago. I hoped that by showing you these pictures you would be able to see how you both resembled each other."

Jonathan stopped eating and examined the photo album closer. His eyes got as big as silver dollar coins. "You mean... you are my grandfather! What! Oh my goodness. I'm really sorry for arresting you now. But if I didn't, we never would have found out about this!" His mind was racing a mile a minute.

Rebecca laughed at her son. She didn't know what else to do. He was taking this so much better than she thought he would. And justifiably so. His mind was so innocent. He had taken everything that they had been through in stride.

"It's ok, no more apologies. I brought you a few of his things and if its ok with your mom I'd like to tell you more about him over breakfast. That is if you can stay a little longer."

"Mom, can we please!"

Looking at her son there was no way that she would break his heart and pull him away. "Yes, we can."

Rebecca stood up and walked to the front door to look out at her vehicle. It was still parked safely like she had last left it when she got their change of clothes out from the car. Snow was still falling from the night before. Everything around the home looked like a winter wonderland. In the distance she could hear

Caleb telling her son all about his father and she wanted to listen in as well, but first she just needed a moment to herself to take this all in.

"Are you ok mom?"

"Yes baby," Rebecca responded finally turning her attention back into their direction. She had lost track of how long she had been standing there. It must have been long enough for Jonathan to take notice. In her mind, she wondered how she would ever be able to pull him away from the closest man he had to his father. How would they go back to the life they knew as vagabonds?

"Rebecca, I hope I am not speaking out of turn and I don't know your whole story, however I have to be honest. I know we just met, but now knowing what we know I cannot allow you and your son to continue with the living conditions you were in. You are family now. I have plenty of room here. I can help you with getting your cellphone on and even looking for a sustainable job to help you get on your feet. I can honestly say that before last night I never knew what I was missing in my life. Now I know it was the two of you. I hope you will allow me to take a role in my grandson's and your life and perhaps we can all help save each other."

She was at a loss for words. Rebecca had not expected that much kindness from what once was a stranger. And she wasn't sure if she could fully accept his offer, but looking at the joy on her son's face and the fact that they were indeed family, how could she decline? In less than twenty-four hours he had done more for them than anyone in her entire family. Perhaps this was the break she had been waiting for, if not for her for her son.

Whatever the future held, this was surely going to be a Christmas that none of them would ever forget.

43

Consequence: Alicia Part One

by Ciara J. Lewis

"Be careful."

I jumped up startled but kept my eyes closed. Ugh. I was never drinking again. Matter of fact, I was done with parties altogether. I don't know why I let my roommate, Alexa, drag me to another party.

No, that wasn't true. I knew exactly why. Knew exactly who I wanted to see. And when I saw them... I should not have gone to that party.

Slowly I rubbed my eyes and thought about the night before. Alexa was hellbent on partying at some frat house. It was holiday themed and everyone was invited. Everyone that was still around during the holiday break anyway.

Our campus was mostly dead. Most students left a few days prior. Alexa didn't have a family to go home to. I just preferred not to go home.

Families are complicated.

I was almost home free until Alexa came with this sad story about Tyson inviting her to the party, which meant we had to go. This was the Tyson she was crushing on. The same Tyson I'd heard about non-stop after the two collided in the hallway and became friends. The same Tyson I had a class with and unfortunately had to listen to him go on about his crush on Alexa.

I was tired of this weird game and told Tyson to make his move. I guess him inviting her to the party was his way. Why I had to be the third wheel one would never know.

Once Alexa and Tyson found each other, the third wheel was on her own. I made myself busy and that's all I can remember at this point. Alexa will have to fill in the blanks whenever she woke up, if she was even here herself.

I heard footsteps walking closer to my door and groaned. Alexa was such a morning person. It had to be no later than six in the morning and here she was walking around like we weren't out all night. Typical.

I just wanted to sleep until New Years. Or maybe until the next semester started. That would be better.

My door opened and I looked up in terror as a strange man stopped abruptly looking down at me with a crazy expression.

"What are you doing in my room?"

"What are you doing in my apartment?"

Wait.

"Your room?"

Fully awake now, I gazed around the room before my eyes returned to the stranger who now leaned against the doorframe waiting for me to answer him as if I were the intruder. Which turned out, I was.

"What am I doing here?"

I rubbed my face, willing my memory to bring back my thoughts to no avail.

"Did you bring me here?"

"I just got here three minutes ago. Maybe you came with my boy, Russell. Russell King. Why he would drop you in my room instead of his…"

Russell King? I didn't know a Russell.

"What's your name, Goldie?"

"Goldie?"

He cracked up as if he made some joke. I didn't find anything funny. I didn't know why I was still entertaining him.

"You know, like Goldilocks. From the story."

"I know the story. Were you at the party last night? Did you and Russell bring me here?"

"Nah, I wasn't there."

"I asked you two questions."

"Like I said, I wasn't there, and I haven't seen Russell. What happened when he brought you here?"

I thought for a moment, begging my mind to clear up just enough to remember Russell. Maybe even remember how I'd gotten here. Or better yet, why I'd come here instead of going home. And where was Alexa? Where was Russell?

It felt like the room was getting smaller as this stranger stared at me with apparently all the patience in the world. He'd asked a question and wanted an answer. An answer I didn't know myself.

"I don't remember coming here."

"You don't..." He stopped himself, shaking his head. "Maybe he went to do something."

"And not come back? Is that like him?"

"Not really, no, but neither is partying."

"Where were you so late at night?"

"Minding my business."

He chuckled but I frowned, not finding any humor in this situation. He wasn't making matters any better.

"I work nights in a grocery store as a second job."

"Why aren't you home for Christmas?"

"This is my home."

"You know what I mean. Like with family or something."

"Same answer. I was born and raised here. What about you?"

I swung my legs letting my feet hit the ground. My eyes glanced around the room again looking for my purse, finding it behind me on the bed. I dug inside until I found my phone. Alexa had called 10 times; my mother calling three. Sighing, I slammed my phone back into my purse.

When I looked up the man was gone from the doorway. I took that as my cue to leave and figure out what in the world happened.

I found him in his living room, his phone to his hear. A moment later, he hit a button and tossed the phone on the couch.

"Russ isn't answering his phone. I'll try him again in a few."

"Thank you."

"Donovan."

"What?"

"My name is Donovan."

We stared at each other for a moment before I looked away.

"I'm gonna head home."

"You didn't answer my question."

"What question?"

Donovan smirked before shaking his head. I knew what question. He didn't need to know the answer.

"Forget it."

"Do you think Russell will be back soon?"

"Hard to say."

"You don't have any answers, do you?"

"I can say the same for you."

He had a point and I was being difficult. Clearly it wasn't his fault that I was here. That didn't stop my nerves from being rattled that I'd blacked out the night before and ended up in this predicament. That was so unlike me.

"I don't remember meeting anyone named Russell. I don't remember much about last night after a certain point honestly."

"I'm sure your memory will come back soon."

One could only hope. I turned towards the door before stopping to look back.

"When you see Russell, can you tell him Ally is looking for him?"

"Ally, huh? Didn't picture that as your name."

That was probably because no one called me that twice to my face. He didn't need to know that. And if I had some sense left in me last night, I would have given Russell the same name.

"Nice to meet you, Ally. Sort of. Do you think you live close by? I can walk you home."

"No, thank you. I've taken up enough of your time. I'm sure you want to get to sleep or whatever."

"You sure?"

I wasn't sure but I didn't want to tell him that. "Please give Russell my message."

2

"Where have you been? I've been looking all over for you?"

Alexa charged at me as soon as I entered the apartment. I pulled away from her, eying Tyson lounging on our sofa as if he'd been there numerous times. I met her eyes again as she realized Tyson was there with her.

"We've been looking for you all morning, Alicia."

"Well, I'm here now so chill."

I left the living room straight to the bathroom and after a half an hour, I still felt a little off. I walked into my room unsurprised to see Alexa sitting on my bed waiting for me.

"Honestly... I woke up in a random apartment." Alexa's eyes bugged out. "Nothing happened"

"How do you know nothing happened?"

I thought about everything and she had a point. Donovan seemed to be telling the truth but who knew at this point.

"Did you call my mother?"

Alexa looked down for a moment before giving me her sad face and I knew she was about to say some bull.

"Look, you weren't answering any of my calls. I needed to know where you were. I thought maybe you changed your mind about going home and so I thought I'd call and see if—"

"Let's stop you right there. You know me and you know that's not an option. How about we go back into the living room so your boyfriend won't be alone."

"He's not my boyfriend."

"Whatever you say, Alexa."

Once I finished dressing, I had to hold my laugh in seeing how close Tyson and Alexa were. She may not have realized it fully but Tyson had claimed her as his.

"So you two seem extra chummy."

"Don't start. I'm not the one who went missing all night. You know how I am. You can't do that to me."

"I know. I'm sorry." I eyed Tyson. "Do you know a guy named Russell King? He was at the party last night."

"Did he do something to you?"

I ignored Alexa's question, staring at Tyson. Maybe it was like Donovan said. Russell dropped me off at his dorm, for safe keeping hopefully, and went about his business to continue his fun on a Friday night.

"No. Tyson?"

"Never heard of him."

I figured I'd give it a shot even though I knew it probably wasn't possible. Unless Russell played on the football team, Tyson probably wouldn't know him.

"Look, I need to get some rest."

"Alicia."

"I'm fine. A little shaken up but I'm okay and safe. That's all that matters."

I went back into my room intending on getting the rest I just said I needed. Then, I heard my phone ringing. When I saw it was my mother again, I hit decline, took a deep breath and hoped this day would not get any worse.

Within seconds, I was reversing my steps and walking out of my room.

"Where are you going?"

"Just... out."

"Do you want me to come with you? Why can't you just stay here? Are you hungry? Tyson can get you something."

I bit back the smile threatening to come out at Alexa's rapid-fire questioning. It was cute when she tried to mother me. Today was not one of those times.

"No, you have company and I need to be alone for a while."

I made it all the way to the doorknob when I heard Alexa call my name. So close.

"Maybe you should call your mom back. She sounded worried about you."

"She's good at acting."

Alexa looked at Tyson who gave me a curious look. Outside of him endlessly sharing his love for Alexa, Tyson and I didn't talk much in class. He didn't know me and I didn't know him. Right now, it was better to keep it that way.

"I'm fine, Alexa."

3

I wasn't fine but if I let Alexa onto that, she'd never let me out of her sight. I couldn't deal with her right now. I needed to be alone with my own thoughts and I knew she'd do nothing but ask countless questions about last night or even worse why I was so adamant about not going home for Christmas.

I drove over to my favorite spot that wasn't too far from campus but far enough that not too many from school ventured this way for something to eat. It was great during the semester when I wanted some time to study and wanted quiet while enjoying a bite to eat.

Today, I needed to remember the night before. That was the only thing on my agenda. Nothing was coming to me and I was beginning to worry. Russell held the keys to the locked memories and he'd literally disappeared into the night.

"Is this seat taken?"

I looked up to see Donovan hovering over my table but far enough to give me space.

"If I hadn't woken up in your room, I'd think you were stalking me."

Instead of waiting for an answer, Donovan slid into the booth across from me. "Or maybe we just like the same spot. Have you ordered yet?"

"No."

"Cool. Breakfast is on me."

"You don't have to do that."

"I want to."

I wasn't going to argue with him, especially when he was offering a free meal. But I couldn't help thinking of how we met. It just all seemed so strange. I didn't know what to make of Donovan. I didn't know whether to believe him or not.

"You're uncomfortable."

It was like he was reading my thoughts. Glancing at Donovan, my intuition told me he was a good guy but to be careful. Those two words were ringing in my head all morning. I was taking heed.

"I am. It's not you—"

"No, no." Donovan laughed, not believing me for a second. "I get it. If I were in your shoes, I wouldn't be the most trusting of me either. It had to be weird waking up and seeing me."

"And in your bed."

"Yeah, I mean Russell's room is further from the front door, but I mean... I guess I get it. Your apprehension, I mean."

"Yeah."

"Have you remembered anything?"

"No."

"Wow. Really? Did you drink that much or are you blocking the memories?"

"Why would I block the memories? Do you know something I should know?"

"I'm gonna say this for the last time. I never saw you before I got back from work. I haven't seen Russ since yesterday morning. We didn't, nor do we, have some crazy plot to kidnap you or anything worse. If anything, Russ probably saved you. That's the type of dude he is."

I nodded slowly. "That thought has run through my mind."

"He's a good guy. Probably just saw you had one too many drinks and wanted to make sure you slept it off."

"I'll have to thank him... if he ever appears."

Donovan was quiet then, making me nervous. His eyes met mine and I saw something unfamiliar. Something vulnerable.

"This isn't like him. Russell... he's more of the loner type. His words, not mine. I'm cool with him mostly 'cause we've been roommates for a couple years. If he isn't on the field practicing or at a game, he's home."

"The field?"

"Yeah, he's a wide receiver on the team. Russ said Coach wanted the team to do some extra practice before their big game in a couple of weeks so that's why most of the team is still here."

I didn't respond, silence falling between us. If he was a wide receiver, that meant Tyson had to know him and lied to my face.

The front door to the diner slammed closed and I jumped at the noise. Suddenly, I was transported back to the night before.

I was sitting on the porch of the frat house before I slowly stood, titling to the left. A guy grabbed me, holding me up straight. He laughed, telling me that I better be careful. I smiled and told him I was just waiting for my ride to go home. He suggested walking me home and moments later we were on our way.

Only halfway there, a gunshot went off. The guy pulled me down into some bushes, looking himself to see if we were in any imminent danger. The sudden movement made me dizzy and I felt like throwing up. He must've known because he put a finger to his lips. Then he was off, leaving me there alone.

A moment later I heard shouting. His was one of the voices, though I was too drunk to make out any of what was being said. I wasn't too drunk to know I'd heard a gunshot and needed to get out of there.

I stood and again stumbled. Again, the man caught me and smiled, telling me to be careful. He told me his apartment was close and if it was okay for us to go there so I could sleep this off. He promised to call me a ride in the morning.

"Ally?"

I blinked, once then twice. Looking around, I was back in the diner. Donovan was sitting across from me, concern etched on his face.

"Do you remember something?"

"Russell."

My thoughts were jumbled. I didn't know what to believe or what my crazed drunkenness had stirred up to confuse me. I told him of what I'd just remembered and Donovan sat there just as perplexed as I was.

"You heard a shot? Did you see anything?"

"I don't think so."

"Why would Russell... who was he arguing with?"

I didn't bother responding since I was sure he was asking himself rather than me.

"Your memory is starting to come back so that's good right?"

"Yes, it is."

"What made you drink so much last night?"

I knew the question was coming. Knew at this point it didn't make sense not to answer. As much as I didn't want to answer, I knew I had to.

"I saw my ex and his current girlfriend."

"Always an ex. What's his name so I can hate him on sight?"

I chuckled at his question. I knew he was being funny but I halfway believed him. I was beginning to like Donovan.

"Wes. We dated about two years."

"Let me guess. He was cheating with his current."

"Nope, he claims to this day that he broke up with me before they got together. He wanted to concentrate on his studies and being tied down was messing with that but he still loved me."

"Bull."

"Pretty much."

I looked down. The memory of that moment replayed in my mind almost every day since it happened over the summer break.

"Do you still love him?"

"Depends on my mood. Right now, I don't. I'm just mad."

"What happened when you saw him last night?"

"He was hugged up in the corner with a girl I had a class with this past semester. She'd been very vocal about her boyfriend and how they'd been dating since the beginning of the semester. She never said a name so imagine my surprise. So much for not wanting to be tied down."

"You thought you'd get back together?"

"I knew we would."

"It's for the better. He sounds like a jerk."

I rolled my eyes at Donovan as he shrugged. "He wasn't a jerk. He just... maybe it was for the best like you said. That's what my roommate tells me when I get down about it."

"She sounds like a good friend."

"She is."

"Was she there last night or went home?"

"She was with me at first." Until Tyson, I added silently.

"Had you drunken anything before seeing Wes?"

"Are you studying psychology or something?"

Donovan shook his head and laughed. "Just curiosity. My dad's a cop so I learned some things from him as far as trying to piece clues together."

"Are you thinking about becoming a cop?"

"We're talking about you."

He was right and I was trying to deflect. I was good at it. Donovan was trying to help me piece my memories back together. Only, the more I told my story and after what I just remembered, the more I wanted to forget.

"After I saw him, I went to the makeshift bar and had about four shots in a row. That got me pretty nice."

"I bet."

My shoulders slumped. I know he meant no harm, but I felt awful about this whole ordeal. Maybe if I would've reacted better to seeing Wes, none of this would've happened. I looked over at Donovan. If last night were different, I wouldn't have met him either.

"So you have two jobs?"

"Gotta pay for the apartment somehow."

"If you weren't working, would have gone to the party last night?"

"I'm not a partygoer."

"Me either."

"Would you like to share why you didn't go home now or you still don't trust me enough?"

I sighed, hoping he wasn't going to loop back to that question. I wasn't lying before when I said it wasn't him.

"I'd rather deal with one problem at a time."

Donovan nodded in agreement as our waiter returned with our food. He was gone just as quickly. I eyed Donovan to see his eyes already on me.

"If you and your friend would like somewhere to eat for Christmas, my mom would welcome y'all with open arms. She loves a full house."

"Even strangers?"

"The more the merrier. Russell's gonna be there, too."

"Is that supposed to make me warm up to the idea?"

Donovan shrugged. "Not really."

"I'll let her know. Alexa doesn't like to cook and I'm not really in the holiday mood. Maybe if her man wants to go."

"Ah, you're not trying to be a third wheel for Christmas."

"Not if they're gonna be boo'd up. I'd rather go home." I sighed again, unintentionally bringing that up and giving Donovan an in to dig deeper.

Instead, he reached into his pocket and grabbed his phone. "I called Russell a few times after you left but I'll try again."

"Maybe he's passed out drunk."

Donovan didn't reply as he listened to his phone. Pressing a button, he put the call on speaker so we both could hear.

"This is the first time it's rung. Maybe you're right about him being passed out."

I hoped I was right, but the more the phone continued to ring, the hope dwindled.

"Hello?"

The voice was groggy but I remembered it. It was Russell.

"Yo, man. Where are you? I've been calling you all morning.

Russell didn't say a word, but we could hear shuffling in the background.

"Russ?"

"My bad, D. What's up?"

Donovan looked at me and I nodded at his silent question.

"The girl you brought to our apartment last night, what happened?"

"Nothing. I mean… she's safe right? She's okay?"

"Yeah, why wouldn't she be?"

Again, Russell didn't answer, making me worry about what else transpired between us meeting on the porch and getting to his apartment.

"I tried to keep her away from what went down." Russell blew out a long breath into the phone and it sent a chill down my spine. "She was pretty drunk, so I don't think she remembers… man, I should've listened to you."

I eyed Donovan but his face scrunched up as if he had no idea what Russell was talking about. I thought I was the only one confused by his cryptic speech.

"Why? What happened?"

"The less you know, the better. Look, I have to go."

"Wait. Ally's looking for you. She wants to know what happened, too."

More shuffling in the background. "D, trust me. If I didn't get her out of there, she would've been witness to something… I don't… listen, we're boys, right?"

"Right."

"So you know me. Just remember that. Remember I tried to be the bigger man. Remember that, D."

"I don't—"

"Tell her I'm sorry but I'm glad she's okay."

"What? Wait."

The phone clicked off and Donovan stared down at it. I watched him for a few moments before grabbing his phone to turn it off. He looked up at me as if realizing I was still there.

"You could've said something, you know?"

"I wouldn't even know what to say. I don't think he would've been able to answer anyway."

Donovan nodded but seemed far away in his thoughts.

"What did he mean? What should he have listened to you about?"

Like before, Donovan was silent for a moment as he thought of an answer to my question. "He wanted off the football team, but he was too afraid to quit. Thought his father would disown him or something. I thought it was ridiculous since he didn't want to play from jump."

"Then why did he?"

"His father's the head coach."

"None of this makes sense."

"I hope whatever has him like this isn't too bad for his sake."

"And mine."

Donovan looked at me with pity in his eyes and I couldn't take it, dropping my gaze. I put my napkin down, no longer hungry.

"I should get going."

"Do you need a ride home?"

"I drove."

Donovan only nodded, digging into his food.

"I don't want you to think—"

"You don't know what I'm thinking."

"That's what's bothering me."

"Because of how we met?"

I only nodded my answer. I watched Donovan reach into his pocket, grab his wallet and toss some money onto the table.

"You don't have to go."

Donovan gave a small smile as he put his wallet back in his pocket.

"No, I do. It was good meeting you, Goldie. I wish we'd met under different circumstances."

Not giving me a chance to respond, Donovan stood from his seat. All I could do was watch him leave. When he got to the front door, he turned slightly to wave. A moment later, he was gone.

4

I went through the weekend seemingly in a trance. I was so glad I didn't have to work and school was on break because I was useless at this point.

I closed my eyes, taking me back to the new memory I'd recovered. I kept playing it back in my head, trying desperately to make sense of it all.

"Get rid of the girl and let's do this."

I didn't recognize the voice but whoever it was was rapidly approaching. Russell walked further from me as I drunkenly hid behind the bushes he dropped me behind.

"Just let me bring her home."

"So you can back out? Nah. Just leave her. We need to go now.

I took a chance, peeking out behind the bushes slightly.

"I just... I don't think we should do this, man."

The other guy sighed, probably in agreement. "Maybe it won't be so bad."

"Come on, Liam. We both know that if we go through with this there's no turning back."

"We don't have a choice."

"Nah, man. It doesn't feel right and I just can't. You know this is wrong."

"But Coach—"

"I can handle him."

The other man, Liam, didn't say a word. I could hear other footsteps coming, about two or three others.

"What's the problem?"

I knew that voice. Wes?

"You shooting at people now?"

Wes, always cocky and seemingly in control, laughed for a moment. "I wouldn't have shot you. It was just a warning."

"I wasn't going anywhere. Just bringing this girl back to her apartment."

"Girl? What girl?"

I heard feet shuffling. It sounded as if Russell was blocking Wes' path from seeing me. It would be just my luck for Wes to see me practically at my worst.

"I don't know her but she's pretty drunk."

"He's chickening out."

"I'm... not. But I am having second thoughts."

I could hear Wes take a step closer to Russell, probably only wanting him to hear what he said next. I pulled my knees close to my chin trying my best to stay hidden.

"What would your father say if he knew you were punking out? We're so close."

"At what cost?"

Wes didn't say anything for a while. I hoped Russell was getting through to him.

"Look, man. We need you. We're in and out in five minutes. Just leave her and let's go. We're running out of time."

"And if I say no?"

"Then the next shot won't miss, you or your girl."

Quickly I covered my mouth before the gasp came out. I felt like screaming. I didn't know this Wes. He was dangerous. He was talking crazy I needed to get out of there.

I watched Russell walk closer to me. The pain in his eyes made me wish he had the power to just leave and not do whatever stupid plan Wes was forcing him to do. But I could see it on his face... whatever they wanted him to do, he was going through with it. He didn't have a choice.

Russell turned again. He must've been thinking of some way to buy time because he was looking down, nervously kicking at the grass.

"My apartment is at the end of the street. Let me drop her off there."

No one said anything for a while. I was afraid they wouldn't agree. What they had to do was clearly more important.

"Ten minutes, Russell. Then you meet us back at the house. You got it?"

Russell nodded quickly. He watched them walk away before hurrying back over to me just as I was standing and stumbling into his arms.

"Hey, be careful."

"I should be saying that to you."

"My apartment is close. Let me bring you there. You'll be safe."

I was hesitant, watching him rub the front of his face clearly frustrated by the events unfolding and how I was now a part of it.

"I'll bring you to my place now and make sure you have a ride back home in the morning. I promise. But we need to go."

"But—"

"Now."

If I were smart, I should have run away the moment Wes and his goons left. Instead, I followed Russell as he led me to his place.

"Stay here. Okay? You'll be safe."

"Safe from what?"

Russell paced back and forth as he rubbed the back of his neck. I was too tired to bother leaving at this point, lying on the bed he'd sat me on.

"Wait."

Russell turned at the door, looking down at me.

"Be careful."

He nodded with a slight smile on his face. "I'll be back."

Those were his last words to me before he closed the bedroom door and a few moments later, the front door. A few minutes later, I was passed out for the night.

I walked out of my room and stopped abruptly seeing Tyson lounging on our sofa.

"Where's Alexa?"

"She went to get some Christmas presents or something. I really don't know. The girl can talk fast sometimes, you know."

He laughed but I kept my face straight, wondering how I wanted to broach this subject with Tyson. He lied about knowing Russell. There was no way they were on the same team, Russell a wide receiver, and Tyson not know him. I knew Wes was on the team, even went to a few games when we dated.

"Is your coach really keeping you over the holiday?"

"Yeah. Well, we had practice yesterday and he's giving us a few days off for Christmas. I'm thinking about catching a quick flight to my grandparents."

"Interesting."

"Why is that?"

"I don't know. I just think it's weird that your coach would just keep you here from your family just for football. I don't get it."

"Maybe it's not for you to get."

"Maybe not. Just like how I don't get how you can say you don't know Russell when he's a wide receiver on your team and his father's the coach."

"Alicia."

"Don't Alicia me, Tyson. You knew I was looking for him and you lied to my face. Don't act like you thought I was talking about someone else either."

He smartly didn't try to deny the truth.

"You knew I was looking for Russell and didn't bother to say anything."

"What would it matter? I haven't seen him since the party."

"You're lying."

Tyson and I shared a look. In my silence, I let him know that I knew more than he thought I knew. My memory had returned.

"I want to forget Friday night. Can we leave it at that?"

"No, Tyson. We can't."

I started back towards my room in frustration since I knew Tyson wouldn't offer anymore. He was hiding something. Russell was missing. And there was no way I was about to ask Wes what was going on.

I looked up to see Tyson hesitantly standing in my doorway.

"What?"

"Did he say anything to you? About Friday night?"

I couldn't believe the gall Tyson had to ask me that question, but I should've figured it. Whatever went down was bad and it looked as if they all were covering their own behinds, Tyson included. A shame since I thought he was one of the good guys.

"He didn't tell me anything." I grabbed my keys off my dresser, walking until I stopped right in front of Tyson. "Don't worry. I won't tell Alexa."

5

I banged my hand on the front door, maybe a little too hard but I didn't care. I needed to speak to Russell or Donovan. It didn't matter who opened the door at this point.

"Ally?"

I stared at Donovan for a moment before I shook my head. "Can I come in?"

Donovan stepped aside, giving me a silent answer. I walked past him to plop down onto the couch. I was so exhausted with all the new information, I didn't know what I was going to do.

"It's Alicia."

"What?"

"My name. It's Alicia. I gave you a fake name. I'm sorry about that. I woke up in a stranger's bed. I didn't know what was going on. I didn't trust you. I didn't—"

"It doesn't matter."

Donovan moved over to sit on the edge of the couch waiting for me to say something. Only at this point, I was tired of everything. I just wanted to sit in silence but I couldn't do that either, too plagued by the returning memories.

"My memory came back."

"Really?"

I nodded sadly. "Not necessarily a good thing. I kind of wish I had blocked it out."

"Why?"

"I found out some information about some people and I just don't... I don't know what to do. Whatever happened Friday, whatever Russell was involved in definitely had something to do with the football team and his father or I don't know."

I quietly gave Donovan a quick rundown of what I remembered. When I finished, I watched him to see his reaction.

"I think Tyson was there that night, too."

"Probably. Are you sure that's what you heard? And Wes, he had a gun?"

All I could do was nod, not believing it myself. "Tyson asked me if Russell said anything to me and Wes said something about them running out of time. What if whatever they did was illegal and if I know—"

"You don't."

"They don't know that. I'm sure Tyson is telling Wes right now. Just what I need."

We were silent for a few minutes. I closed my eyes before turning my gaze towards Donovan.

"Were you serious before? About Alexa and I coming over for Christmas dinner?"

"Sure, why not?"

"Because you don't know us."

"Only if you want to."

"My mother... she recently remarried. Apparently, he was her high school sweetheart. She was the one that got away. Went to college and fell in love with another man, my father. My dad." I stopped to take a breath because I hated telling this story, but I needed to get it out. "He passed a few years ago but Christmas... that was his time. He loved it. Started decorating the moment Thanksgiving was over. It'll be five years tomorrow since he died." I closed my eyes at the memory. "This year her husband thought it would be a good idea for a big Christmas dinner between him, my mom, me and his four kids. I wasn't having it. My mom is obviously upset but I just… it feels like disrespect to my father and I can't bring myself to go home even if I wanted to."

"Do you want to?"

I almost forgot Donovan was there for a moment. Shaking myself, I shrugged. "I'm not sure. It would be good to see my mom. They eloped over the summer so I didn't see her then. And that's when the whole thing went down with Wes, so I wasn't trying to see anybody anyway."

"Okay, well you definitely have to come to my parents' home for dinner."

"Why?"

"Because my mom is just as crazy about Christmas as I'm sure your father was. I think it'll give you some comfort."

"Maybe."

A loud banging on the door stopped our conversation just when I was starting to feel an inch better. Donovan walked to the door opening it. The older man on the other side wasted no time barging inside.

"Where's Russell?"

"He's not here. Hasn't been all weekend."

As if not believing Donovan, the man continued further into the apartment, walking back towards the bedrooms. I watched Donovan as he kept his eyes on the man. He didn't seem bothered by the intrusion so I wouldn't either.

The man reentered the living room, a stricken look on his face. "Have you talked to him? His phone keeps going to voicemail. I need to talk to him."

"Not since yesterday. He sounded out of it to be honest."

"Yeah, I bet."

As if realizing I was there, the man looked down at me way longer than I felt comfortable before returning his eyes to Donovan.

"If you see Russell before I do, tell him to come home."

"What's going on?"

"Don't question me! You just give him my message. Got it?"

Donovan and the man stared at each other before the man grunted and started for the door.

"Who was that?"

"Russell's father."

"The coach."

My phone vibrated and I took it out of my pocket, not recognizing the number. The message sent chills down my spine though.

"What is it?"

"Keep your mouth shut or you're next."

"Next for what?"

Before I could respond, my phone rang to Alexa's unmistakable ringtone. "I'm a little busy, Lex."

"Come home, now. It's not safe."

"What are you talking about?"

"They found someone. Tyson just told me."

I looked at Donovan as he impatiently waited for me to get off the phone. I took the phone from my ear and put it on speakerphone. "Who did they find?"

"I don't know. Tyson?"

I heard some mumbled voices until Tyson cleared his throat. "I don't know the details. My boy said some guy was jumped."

I looked at Donovan and I could tell we shared the same thought. Tyson was lying again. He knew way more than he was telling.

"Okay well I'm safe, Alexa."

"You don't get it. They're saying Russell had something to do with it. The same Russell you were looking for. Tyson's friend said they saw the victim and Russell arguing at the party Friday before he left."

"What does that have to do with me?"

"I don't know. You saw Russell that night. Do you remember him arguing with anyone?"

Liam. Wes. Probably Tyson. Probably whoever this friend was of Tyson.

"Do you have the name of the victim?"

"Not yet. He was just found like an hour ago."

"Where?"

Donovan stood at the same time as me, both of us silently heading to the door.

"At the park close to the frat house we were at."

"Lex, I gotta go."

"Alicia."

"I'll call you later."

I hung up the phone to see Donovan holding the doorknob. "What are you thinking?"

"We need to find Russell."

6

The cold air didn't stop the determination in my steps. Donovan and I had been walking silently for a while. He mentioned checking the campus, so we were on our way.

"If your offer still stands, I'd like to have dinner at your parents' place. I'm sure Alexa will, too."

Donovan glanced my way but didn't say anything, just kept walking but with a noticeable smirk on his face. I rolled my eyes, my face spreading into its own smile.

"You trust me now?"

"I wouldn't equate trust with a free meal."

"Fair enough. I understand why you don't wanna go home."

"Would you if you were in my shoes?"

"Maybe. I don't know. You have a right to feel how you feel. So does your mom. It's an unfortunate situation all around. You're not ready for the big family thing. You'll feel like you're forgetting your father or letting him go."

"How do you do that? Be in my head?"

"Just piecing clues together."

We made it to the campus and immediately saw a small group starting to form. We looked at each other before making our way over. Halfway there, we heard a loud scream and before I knew it, Donovan and I broke out into a full sprint over. Donovan moved his way through the crowd, but I stayed back on the outskirts observing.

Some students had their faces down. Some were fully crying. A few down on their knees in visible pain. I even saw one kid looking like he was about to lose his lunch.

After a few minutes, Donovan emerged from the group as I heard the faint sound of sirens. He hunched down, whatever he saw hitting him hard. My feet moved over to Donovan, touching him on the shoulder as I bent down in front of him.

"Donovan?"

"Just give me a minute."

As the sirens continued to grow louder, I took it upon myself to leave Donovan and head into the crowd myself.

I couldn't help the gasp as I saw Russell's lifeless body lying on the ground. I looked up and could put two and two together. Either he'd jumped from the roof or he'd been pushed.

I walked back out just as the ambulance raced to park in front of where we were gathered. Donovan was in the same spot, hunched over. Unbelief on his face.

He looked up at me as if feeling my presence. "Russell wouldn't kill himself."

I kneeled down in front of Donovan, making sure no one was within earshot. "What if this has to do with Friday night? With the other person who's... remember he said he tried to be the bigger man? This has to do with that. Right?

Donovan stood then, holding his hand out for me to do the same. We walked a short distance before Donovan stopped and looked back.

"Tyson knows something. I bet your boy, Wes, does too."

I thought about the text I received. Either Wes or Tyson sent that message and I didn't know how to take that information. I looked up at the building and could have sworn I saw a shadow moving. I went to ask Donovan when I saw someone running quickly across the field.

The coach. Russell's father. I may have been uncomfortable and unnerved in the one meeting we'd had but his son was on the ground dead.

"Let's go back to my place," I offered.

"You sure?"

I nodded my answer as we turned back and headed in the direction of my apartment. I could see it in Donovan's eyes. He didn't want to go anywhere near his place. It would just remind him of Russell. It was the last place he needed to be right now.

7

Usually I had a problem with the cold but after the last week, I welcomed the uncomfortable feeling settling over me as I sat on the porch.

I was numb. Two dead students on campus within 24 hours. It was a living nightmare.

The news was reporting that the first victim, Carter Walls, was killed by a blunt object. There were no suspects at this time. I knew what that meant. Everyone thought Russell did it and since he'd committed suicide, supposedly, there was no reason to keep Carter's case open.

It was all fishy to me.

"You okay?"

I looked up and then away as my mother stood at the top of the porch. Alexa forced me to go home. She said there was no way she was staying around on holiday break during whatever this was. So even though I did not want to come home, I let Alexa talk to me into both of us coming here. I asked her about Tyson, but she mumbled something about him ghosting her, so I let the conversation go.

"Alexa tells me you met a boy."

"I wouldn't say that."

I watched my mother sit next to me. If only Alexa really knew what was going on. She'd probably tried to stage a coup about never stepping foot anywhere near our college again.

"I miss him, too, you know. Your father. I miss him every day. I don't want you to think that I just moved on. Weston must've asked me for six months to marry him before I finally accepted that I was in love with him, too."

That was another point of contention for me. Every time I heard the man's name, it reminded me of my ex. The same ex I was convinced directly threatened me. I hadn't received any more text messages but the timing of it was no coincidence. Tyson wasn't that dumb. Liam didn't know me. Wes was the only one bold enough to send that message knowing I wouldn't say anything… yet.

"I know you don't understand that, but I need you to be okay with this, Alicia. I need you to—"

"Mom, I really don't… I get it, okay. I'm happy that you're happy. I'm happy you found love with Weston. I'm not mad. I'm just not ready. I'm not there. It's not you. It's not him. It's me. I need to get to the place where I can be around you two and not feel like a piece of me is dying inside. Trying to do that during Christmas probably isn't the best time."

"I know. I told Weston we need to be patient."

"I'm here now so…"

"But you don't want to be."

I wasn't going to confirm or deny that, but she was right. I may have been there in body, but my mind was still back on campus. Back with wondering what happened. Back with what caused Russell to jump or be pushed. I needed to know the truth.

My eyes met my mother's and she had a small smile on her face. She reached into her pocket, taking out some keys. My keys.

"Mom."

"I don't know what's going on, but I suspect this is more than about us. Don't worry about Alexa. By the time she realizes you left, you'll be halfway home."

"Doesn't mean she won't call me a thousand times."

"She won't. I'll make sure of it. Go back and settle whatever it is bothering you."

I took my keys and my purse that she'd also somehow smuggled out the house before giving her a tight hug.

I was going back and starting a journey into who knows what but it's something I had to do. I already knew where my first stop would be.

"Alicia?"

I gave a small smile as I stood in front of Donovan at his apartment. There was no point of going back to my place when I knew I needed to see him first. I needed to know he was okay. I'd only just met Russell, but Donovan knew him. He was his roommate. He was his friend. I felt his pain.

"What are you thinking?"

I met Donovan's gaze as I mulled over his question. "We need some answers."

"Who first?"

"Wes."

Donovan had his coat on and was at the door within what seemed like seconds. He looked back at me as I stood in the middle of his living room.

"You coming or what?"

To Be Continued...

Did you enjoy this book? Please consider leaving a review on Amazon or Goodreads!

About the Authors

Essence Magazine Best Selling Author Nikkea Sharee has been a multimedia force for over a decade. Her award winning novels span a variety of genres from drama, romance, murder mystery, poetry and even young adult fiction. A noted spoken word artist, she has performed on stages from NY to LA. Now an award winning filmmaker she has founded a company Kweli Legacy with her sister which specializes in short films and documentaries.

Connect with Nikkea via FB, Twitter and Instagram @NikkeaSharee.

Ciara J. Lewis is an author from Connecticut. She is also a filmmaker and co-founder of the production company Kweli Legacy, LLC with her sister, Nikkea Greene. To stay up to date with Ciara, like her Facebook page or follow her on Instagram @ciarajewel.